trogg trouble

Retro Whimsy
Book Two

sabrina cross

author's note

This is a sentient object romance. Humans will be getting it on with sentient objects. Don't worry, everyone is gleefully consenting.

If you read the last three sentences and think that's not for you, that's okay. There is still time to put this book down and walk away. No one will blame you. It's the sane thing to do.

But if you're going to stick around please be aware of the following: body size discomfort, body shaming parent, 2000's diet culture, abandonment issues, feelings of loneliness, family trauma with parents and grandparents. Oral and vaginal sex, sex with sentient objects.

If you feel I am missing anything please reach out to me at authorsabrinacross@gmail.com and let me know. A complete list can be found at www.sabrinacross.com

one

. . .

"Happy birthday!" My best friend Aubry dropped a kraft gift bag on my desk as she passed on the way to her own.

"It's not my birthday." I pointed out. It wasn't even close to my birthday. My birthday wasn't until November, and it was only late June.

Aubry waved that away with a flick of her wrist over her head as she settled in. Our office was a small, open-concept space that was nice when we wanted to chat during the day but annoying when we were both on the phone or trying to get stuff done. There was a guy who worked part-time in accounting that had a desk across from mine, but it was just the three of us in the large room that had once housed nearly a dozen drones.

I tilted the bag toward me and peeked in but could only see the tissue paper sticking out of the top. I was trying not to let curiosity get the better of me. Knowing Aubry, the contents of that bag could be absolutely anything. I wouldn't put it past her to give me a new vibrator in the office.

Which honestly, would be fair turnabout after I

gave her a breakup gift of vibrating panties a couple years ago. She'd opened the bag with our boss standing in the doorway, and you'd have thought the box caught fire. Or her face.

So, obviously, I was a little wary of the gift.

"It's SFW. Just open it." Aubry called over her shoulder as she logged into her computer for the day.

With a sigh, I tugged the white and gold tissue paper out of the bag and looked inside. And then I just sat and stared at the contents for a long moment without moving.

"Do you like them?" Aubry's voice was a little hesitant. When I looked up at her, she had a grin on her face. "I went back to Retro Whimsy this weekend and they were still there, calling your name."

I looked down at the two Trogg dolls in the bag, and a burning sensation clogged my throat. There was no way Aubry could have known what these dolls meant to me as a kid or how hard it would hit me to see them. Especially these two dolls together.

Carefully, I pulled out the little ugly toys. Trogg dolls were made of a soft, rubbery plastic. They all had stumpy arms and legs and rounded bellies. Each doll also had fluffy hair roughly as tall as the body itself. They'd come in a rainbow of colors, but the two in front of me were light blue and deep purple. Just like the ones I'd had as a kid.

I looked down into their glassy black eyes and sardonically smiling faces and fought back tears. There was no way Aubry could have known which two to pick. There had been a group of them at the vintage shop when we'd gone before. But somehow, she gave me the two I'd had as a girl and had lost.

"I love them," I say through the lump in my throat. "Thank you."

two

. . .

I let myself into my apartment and dropped my keys onto the side table. Kicking off my shoes, I left them in the hallway before heading straight to my bedroom. I dropped my bag over the back of the couch on my way through the living room but kept the gift bag with my Trogg dolls with me.

I'd tried to talk Aubry into getting dinner with me, but she said she had a date. Which was news to me since I didn't even know she was looking, let alone dating. She said it just kind of happened but wouldn't give me details. It was so unlike her to be tight-lipped with me.

It definitely raised some red flags, but I couldn't exactly call her out at work. So I'd gone home, alone, to a frozen pizza and half-finished bottle of wine. Maybe I should start dating again.

After changing into a pair of biker shorts and an oversized t-shirt, I pulled the Troggs out of the bag and held them in my hands. There had been a whole collection of Troggs at the store when we'd gone last week. It was eerie how Aubry had known which two colors to get for me.

Of course, she didn't know. How could she? There was no way for her to know the impact of these two particular dolls. I'd never told her about the things I'd had to leave behind when I was a small child.

Oh, she knew about my teenage mother and the battle she'd had with her parents. How it ended with my mom packing me up in the middle of the night and leaving her home and family behind. But I didn't tell her how heartbreaking it had been when Mom wouldn't let me bring anything but my clothes. How scary it had been to be woken up in the middle of the night and carried out to the already loaded car.

She didn't know about the Trogg dolls that had been my constant companions or the secrets I'd told them. She didn't know that for a long while those dolls had been the only friends I'd had. They were my family and safe harbor in the chaos that was life with my mom and grandparents.

Blinking back tears, I set the dolls on my bedside table. I didn't want to go down the rabbit hole of my childhood. I just wanted to enjoy the nice gift my friend had given me because she'd been thinking of me. Holding that thought close, I left the bedroom.

In the kitchen, I poured myself a large glass of wine and reheated the pizza I'd had for dinner the night before. I didn't really want either, but I was feeling edgy and restless and needed to do something.

For a brief moment, I thought about grabbing my bag and putting my gym membership to use but came to my senses before I even got my shoes on. Nothing good ever came from going to the gym in the evenings with the after-work crowd.

Finally, I settled myself onto the couch with a comfort movie playing in the background and decided to combat the loneliness by re-downloading a dating app and setting up a new profile. Two hours of swiping later, I'd remembered why I deleted the app in the first place. The men I did match with either didn't message back or had the conversational skills of a rock. And the only women the app showed me were looking for thirds in their marriages. No shade to polyamorous people, but I did not want to join some long established marriage that was probably on the rocks and looking to spice things up in a vain attempt to save it.

Been there. Done that. Have the t-shirt I claimed after the dude ripped the strap of my cami. So not going down that road again.

Not even six months of total celibacy was enough to make me consider it.

After giving up on the idea of getting a date, and the day in general, I rinsed my glass and plate off and left them in the sink to be tomorrow's Cinder's problem and got ready for bed.

Did I feel kind of pathetic going to bed just after eight? Yep. Was I bummed that I hadn't gotten a single update from Aubry on her date? Absolutely. But I was bored, and nothing was keeping my attention. Sleep seemed like the best plan, as lame as that was.

three

. . .

I don't care what anyone says, Tuesdays are worse than Mondays. I crawled out of bed Tuesday morning and stumbled into the shower. Partly the mostly-full bottle of wine I'd consumed the night before and partly due to the weird dreams I'd had.

The shower washed most of the fog away, and an energy drink would do the rest. I wrapped myself in a towel and headed to the kitchen to grab one before getting dressed. Double win of air drying my body a little before pulling on stockings and getting caffeine in my system.

Why hadn't they invented a caffeine IV drip yet?

I popped the top on the drink and leaned back against the counter for the first zippy sip. I froze, my drink halfway to my mouth when I spotted the empty sink. I'd been pretty tired and out of it the night before, but I was almost positive I'd left my dishes in the sink.

Even if I hadn't, I never dry my dishes, and the dish rack was also empty. I sat the drink down and opened the cabinets. There they were, all of my dishes clean and put away where they belong. Which is not a thing that happens with me.

Had I been sleepwalking? It seemed ridiculous that I would clean in my sleep, but weirder things had happened. I glanced at the microwave clock and swore.

I put aside the questions about my suddenly clean kitchen; grabbed my drink and rushed to the bedroom to get ready to go.

I was going to be late.

———

"How was your date last night?" I asked Aubry, as I set an iced coffee on her desk. Was the sugary coffee a bribe for details? Abso-fucking-lutely.

"Amazing." She sighed and gave me a dreamy smile that screamed 'I got laid last night' in neon letters. "How was your night?"

"I downloaded a dating app." I moved past her desk back to mine. "And deleted it again this morning."

"Oh," She sounded disappointed, and I understood why. We'd promised each other months ago that we were done with dating apps. They were so toxic, and nothing good ever came from them.

"I was hoping for something more exciting for you." She said as she spun her chair around to look at me.

"You could tell me about your date and let me live vicariously through you." I didn't like that my bestie was holding back on me. She was more than just a co-worker and work wife. She was my best friend, and she was keeping the dirty details from me. We always shared the good, the bad, and the downright ugly of our dating lives.

"Maybe later." Her smile was so satisfied I could have kicked her, if we weren't at the office.

Nine hours later, Aubry still refused to give up the goods. She also refused to go out to dinner with me, begging off because she was tired from her date. Bragging bitch.

Instead of going home to my empty apartment and another night of streaming bad tv, I took myself out to dinner at the patio bar I liked halfway between work and home. I sat on the patio and read my book on my phone as I ate. I lingered a little, but it was still only seven when I got home.

Walking into my empty, dark apartment, I had to admit the truth. I was lonely. It wasn't the bone-deep, soul-crushing loneliness I'd once felt as a kid, but it was creeping in. I'd never minded being on my own, but something about Aubry dating someone new made me realize how empty my life was.

I had always been a loner and didn't make friends easily. Most of my more casual friends were married or moved or had busy careers they loved. I worked customer service for a company I enjoyed, but it wasn't my end goal. I didn't even have a career goal, just working to pay my bills and spending the rest of my time hanging out with my best friend.

Maybe it was time to find a hobby. Or figure out what I wanted to do with my life. Or got a cat. Cats were great companions. All the spinsters said so.

I dropped my sweater and bag over the back of the couch and kicked off my shoes behind it before heading to my bedroom to change into a pair of silky pants and a cropped cami set I'd gotten myself for my last birthday but never wore because it felt too nice to waste just lounging around the house.

But I was having a pity party, and there was no reason I shouldn't look cute while doing it. In fact, it might have made me feel just a little bit better.

After changing, I padded barefoot into the kitchen to grab a glass of water and a bag of cookies. I took my goodies back to my bed with me and turned on the television to a romcom from the aughts.

I must have fallen asleep because the next thing I know, I'm waking up in the dark.

The television was off.

I sat up, surprised to find myself tucked under the blankets and searched around for my phone only to find it plugged in on my nightstand.

"Okay? What the fuck?"

I used the flashlight on my phone to scan my room and came up empty. Nothing seemed out of place, but I was certain someone had been in my room. I had never been the sleepwalking type, and I knew damn well that my phone hadn't been plugged in.

A wooden baseball bat was tucked behind the bedroom door. I'd never played baseball, but my mom had sworn by them as personal protection items. I'd had one in my bedroom for as long as I could remember. I swung the bat onto my shoulder and tucked the phone into my waistband, using the grip to hold it in place with the flashlight still out so I could see as I walked.

I needn't have bothered since every light in the apartment was on.

And there, in the middle of my living room wielding a broom, was the blue-haired Trogg. Except this doll wasn't eight inches high. It was roughly six feet and its hair was being compressed by the ceiling.

"Oh, hello." It said in a low, rumbling voice.

As though that were the most normal thing in the world. As though a six-foot-tall Trogg doll was completely normal and not at all bonkers.

I did the only thing I could do in that situation. I ran back to my room and locked the door.

four

. . .

"That wasn't real. I'm hallucinating. Or having an allergic reaction. Maybe someone drugged my dinner and the effects are just now hitting me." I paced the room, going over every possible option other than the idea that I had really just seen a giant Trogg doll.

I spun around to look at my bedside table, but the dolls were both gone. Of course they were. Because they were walking around in human-sized bodies cleaning my apartment.

Sure. Totally. Made perfect sense.

I started laughing. Large, full-bodied laughter that rang through the room and carried a distinct note of hysteria to it.

There was a knock on the door. I spun to look at it and watched in horror as it swung open. Of course it did. The lock on the door had been faulty since the day I'd moved into the little apartment.

Both Trogg dolls stood in the open doorway.

"So, you seem a little freaked out." The purple-haired doll said in a crisp tone totally at odds with her casual words.

"Oh, only a little?" I giggled again, it was high and unhinged. I was totally fucking freaked out.

"I think she's going to pass out." Purple says to Blue.

"I think she's made of sterner stuff than that," Blue looked at me, "Aren't you sweetheart?"

Nope. Actually, I didn't think I was. I think I was a moment away from passing out, if the greying around the edges of my vision was anything to go by. My heart was racing so fast it felt like it was vibrating in my chest.

"It's okay, sweetheart. We're not here to hurt you." Blue's voice was calm and soothing, like he was talking to a wild animal.

"Couldn't if we wanted to," Purple was far less soothing. I don't think I liked Purple. Purple would kill me in my sleep if I gave her a chance.

"Not helping, Amethyst," Blue said, shoving her back behind him. "So, here's the deal, we're not going to hurt you. We have no interest in hurting you. We're actually hoping you can help us."

"Help you?" I repeated dumbly.

"Yes, exactly." The doll's smile widened and became even creepier than before. Matched with the dead black eyes, I did the sane thing and took a step back and away. And then I took a couple more until my bed separated us.

"Running away is a sign she doesn't believe you," the purple one, Amethyst, said.

"It's a sign she's bright and wary. It's okay." Blue continued to smile at me. "I'm Cy, this is my friend Amethyst."

I laughed. Right. What else would a purple and cyan blue doll be called?

"And you are?" Again, with the soothing,

talking to a wild animal that wants to bite your face off voice. Honestly, it was kind of grating.

"Oh, my god Cy." Amethyst pushed forward until she stood in front of him. They were the same size, identical in all ways except for their hair and their voices. "She's not brain damaged."

Amethyst looked at me, her eyes blank glass orbs of horror. She propped her hands on her hips and stared me down.

"We pissed off a witch. She cursed us to live in service of others. Once upon a time we were a broom and a feather duster but then something happened a while ago and we got transformed into these forms. We've been stuck this way for years. And now you have us and we're living-ish again. Which means maybe you're the one to break this hellish curse."

"Curse?" I repeated. God, I sounded like an idiot, but my brain was not processing what was happening. How could it?

"Yes, a curse. Very good." Her tone was condescending enough to snap me out of my fugue state.

"Look lady, you've had time to deal with this shit. I've had all of five minutes. Drop the bullshit and let me think!" I snapped at her. She grinned back at me. It was just as terrifying as Cy's smile, but hers was definitely more pleased.

"Oh yay, you do have a spine in there." She clapped her hands together like a child. "I'd say take all the time you need but we don't know how long this will last. Maybe we can stay like this forever and spend every night cleaning your house, maybe we only have a couple of days. We don't know. So, maybe give us some jobs that will make your life easier and we can try to solve your problems and maybe it will break the curse."

"That's a whole lot of maybes." I pointed out.

"It's not like there's a goddamn instruction manual. We're just guessing here. That's all we can do."

Cy put a hand on Amethyst's shoulder, and the purple Trogg took a deep breath before nodding once.

"Sorry. You're right. We'll give you some time." She allowed herself to be pulled out of the room. Cy paused long enough to give me what I think was supposed to be an encouraging smile before he pulled the door closed behind him.

At the click of the latch, my legs gave out and I fell to the bed.

What the fuck was that?

———

My first instinct was to call Aubry. Because I called Aubry with everything. But what could she possibly do? She probably wouldn't even believe me. I mean, it was absolutely crazy.

I sat on my bed and picked at a frayed edge of the comforter for a long moment, trying to sort out my thoughts. First, I chose to believe that they were real. Because it was either that or I probably did go crazy, and I didn't feel particularly crazy. Though, I supposed most crazy people probably didn't feel crazy while having hallucinations either.

But still, it was easier to believe in the impossible.

Second, they needed my help. And while they weren't the same dolls from my childhood, they were Troggs, and Troggs had kept me sane as a little girl. It felt like paying it forward to help them.

Third, I had no clue how to help them. I lived a

comfortable little life. I made enough to cover my bills and essentials and the occasional splurge. My apartment was small but cozy, and it wasn't particularly messy. I wasn't a clean person, but I wasn't messy either. My apartment was lived in.

Honestly, the only thing missing from my life, the only problem I had, was the creeping loneliness and current horniness. And how could they possibly help me with that?

After a long while, I got to my feet and took a steadying breath to face the giant dolls in my living room. There was no noise coming through the door, and for a moment I hoped I had imagined it all. That it had been a very lucid dream. But the moment I opened the door, all hope was dashed.

Cy was in my kitchen organizing my cupboards in some method I didn't understand, while Amethyst was cleaning my windows. Neither were tasks that needed to be done, but I supposed if it made them feel better I wouldn't complain. Maybe doing small tasks would break their curse. I had no way of knowing. The whole concept was frankly crazy.

Both of them looked at me when I came out. I offered a little wave I immediately regretted. Why was I so awkward?

Cy waved back, which made me feel a little bit better. Amethyst just stared at me expectantly. I guessed I couldn't blame her. If I'd been cursed to be a doll servant and had a chance to break it, I'd be pretty impatient too.

I took a deep breath and did the crazy thing.

"I'll help you."

five

. . .

"*H*ey guys, I'm home!" I drop my keys into the bowl on the side table and kick off my shoes in the hall closet. I put my bags on the hook in the closet and sighed. While having a perfectly clean apartment was nice, I kind of missed just dropping things as I went. I wasn't wired to be an "everything in its place" person. But I also felt like shit when Cy and Amethyst went around cleaning up after me, so I made sure to put in the effort.

I moved into the living room and spotted the Troggs on the kitchen counter where I'd left them that morning. Neither responded, but I didn't expect them to.

As far as we could tell, the curse put them into stasis until sundown. At that point, they had the choice to remain small or take their large forms. At sunrise, they went back into their small doll forms. They could see and hear, which is why they were in the kitchen and not my bedroom, but they couldn't do anything until the sun went down.

Honestly, it sounded like Hell to me. Cy assured me it wasn't that bad. Amethyst insisted that it had been worse before, when they'd been cleaning sup-plies. At least now they could move around and interact. Which was just sad.

"I got the chicken and veggies but I'm pretty sure I'm going to mess it up." Amethyst had yelled at me the night before, after watching me eat frozen dinners and take out every day for a week.

Mom hadn't cooked much or well. And I never cared to learn after I moved out. Grandma had been a good cook, and anything related to her was com-plicated at best. But Cy and Amethyst insisted it wasn't as hard as I made it out to be, and we'd picked out an easy enough looking meal to start with.

Not that they could or needed to eat. But, after I got past the fear I would burn my apartment down, I was kind of excited to try. Just so I could say I did it, at the very least.

I carried my grocery bags into the kitchen and put away the cold items, leaving the rest on the counter. Something that would annoy the Troggs endlessly but since they couldn't do anything about it, I left it.

Rude? Maybe a little. I needed out of my work clothes. Summer was really starting to hit, and while the office had air conditioning, it was enough to melt a person just getting from the office to the car. And my car was not new or nice enough for decent AC.

I balled my hair up on top of my head and se-cured it with a clip before taking a quick shower to rinse off the sweat. After drying off, I pulled on a pair of cotton shorts and a sports bra. I was halfway to the kitchen before I remembered the Troggs. Nor-mally, I would never wear something like that in front of other people. I had long ago accepted I would never be a small person, but I still didn't wear clothes that showed off every dip and wrinkle of my thighs and the way my belly jiggled with every movement.

I stood frozen halfway across the living room for a long moment before deciding it would draw more attention to myself if I turned around and changed than if I just wrapped myself in some false confidence. I didn't exactly throw my shoulders back and strut, but I did move with purpose across the apartment to the kitchen.

"Okay guys, let's try not to burn the building down, okay?" I pulled the rest of the ingredients for my dinner out of the bags. I had fresh broccoli, small yellow potatoes, baby carrots, and a host of herbs and seasonings. They had cost a small fortune for something I'd likely never use again.

I kept up a steady chatter with the Troggs as I washed the veggies, cut the chicken breasts into tenders-sized slices, and added the seasonings to everything before I put it in the oven to cook. It was nice to have company, even non-responsive company. It made the time go by as I cleaned up while my dinner cooked.

"I think you might be right about this," I said to the Troggs as I removed the pan from the oven and fragrant steam billowed up into my face. "This smells amazing."

In no time, I had chicken and veggies on a plate and paired it with a glass of white wine. Normally, I either ate standing in the kitchen or sitting on the couch, but I decided that real food deserved a better setting and pulled out one of the rarely used bar stools.

It felt a little weird sitting by myself eating a real meal. With a mom who couldn't cook and worked two jobs, I'd never been a dinner table person. And doing it alone just felt a little sad.

"I wish you could join me," I said to the Troggs. Of course, they didn't answer. It was still hours until sunset.

The food was delicious and better than I had ever imagined I could make. I would have to give Amethyst props for the recipe choice when she woke up. A part of me was tempted to call my mom and tell her about it, but I kiboshed that idea. Mom and I were close, but I knew she had a lot of regrets about the way she raised me. And my tremulous relationship with food was high on that list.

Plus, I avoided talking about anything that had to do with my weight. Mom was a slender woman and had always believed my poor diet led to my weight gain in my teen years. She didn't under-stand that my thyroid barely functioned, and even with medication my metabolism was trash. She just insisted if I ate differently and exercised more everything – my weight – would be just fine in the end.

I didn't blame her, not really. She was a product of her time, while I had somehow escaped the worst of the aughts diet culture, my mom was a permanent victim of it.

Shaking off bad thoughts and memories, I fin-ished my dinner. I put the rest of the food in the fridge for leftovers, but I left the dishes in the sink. I'd gotten better about cleaning up after myself when the Troggs arrived, but they yelled at me if I didn't leave them stuff to do. And honestly, a yelling six-foot Trogg doll was kind of terrifying.

Sometimes I wonder how very lonely I must have been as a kid to have turned the creepy looking things into my confidants. Childhood me was a little unstable. Then again, adult me had two life-size Trogg dolls waiting on me, so I couldn't exactly say I was any more stable now.

Dinner done and put away, I refilled my wine and took it with me into the living room where I turned on a movie and waited for the Troggs to wake up.

six

. . .

"What happens if the curse doesn't break? You've been waiting on me hand and foot for over a week and nothing is changing."

"It has to be you," Amethyst said from behind me. She pulled a brush through my hair in steady, soothing strokes. "There has to be a reason we're here with you."

"You said yourselves, it's been almost exactly a hundred years since the curse was cast. Maybe it's wearing off."

"I don't think magic works that way." Cy said from the other end of the couch where he was rubbing my feet. I'd argued against both things, but they insisted.

Their insistence only made me more determined to break the curse. I couldn't believe they liked doing these things for me. They were only doing what they could to break the curse. And while it was nice to be pampered and spoiled a little, and I enjoyed waking up to a fresh pot of coffee and a clean apartment, it didn't sit right with me; they were only doing it because they had to.

Amethyst and Cy were becoming my friends, in a weird way. I wanted them to want to be with me, not just here because they had no other choice. The other side of that coin was the fact I wouldn't survive loving another set of Trogg dolls only to lose them again.

Childhood trauma is a bitch.

"Think, Cinder, what is it you really need? How can we best serve you?" Cy asked. His thick hands slid up and down my calves, massaging the muscles there. I bite back a moan.

Part of me wants to say it's just that the message feels good, but it isn't just that. I try to remember the last time I'd been with another person. Months? Almost a year? Longer?

Amethyst's hands dive into my hair, and her blunt fingers rub at my scalp. My head lolled forward and this time, the moan slipped out.

"Does our pretty girl need to be touched?" Amethyst asked against my neck. "You were looking for a date when we got here but you haven't gone out once since we arrived."

Her hands slid down my scalp to massage my neck and shoulders. Cy's hands crept back up my legs to knead my thighs. His hands were so large they almost wrapped halfway around. His thumbs dipped down between my clenched legs to rub circles against my inner thighs.

"Oh, I think you're right, Amethyst. She's practically vibrating." Cy pulled one of my legs up so he could kiss the inside of my ankle.

I shuddered under the brush of his lips. A movement that ramped up when Amethyst's mouth dropped to the sensitive curve of my neck. I gripped the couch cushion and tried to get my wits about me.

The night had taken a turn I hadn't expected, and I wasn't sure how to process it. Their hands on me felt great. I'd been craving touch for so long I'd almost forgotten what it could feel like. But at the same time, it felt wrong. Once again, they were just trying to serve my needs, whether they really wanted to or not.

I pulled away from them and scrambled off the couch. I pulled my shorts legs down as far as they could go to cover as much of my legs as possible. Then I crossed my arms over my belly, trying to hide behind them. I didn't just feel unclothed, I felt totally stripped bare.

My skin still tingled from their touch, and my body throbbed with want. But there was no way I could take what they offered and not feel guilt.

"I'm sorry, I can't." I backed up a few steps and stumbled over the corner of a coffee table before moving clear of the furniture so I could make a hasty escape to my room.

I closed the door and threw myself against it as I tried to catch my breath. I was a terrible person. The Troggs depended on me to help them, and they were willing to do anything, including me, to get free of their curse.

"Cinder, can I come in?" Cy's voice was deep on the other side of the door. I shook my head but pushed away from the door to allow him to open it.

"We're sorry," Cy said as he slid in the small gap between the door and the frame. "We pushed too hard and frightened you. We shouldn't have done that."

Cy shoved his broad hands into the giant poof of hair on his head and winced when they got tangled in the coarse strands. I fought back a sympathetic wince as he slowly worked his fingers free of the blue cotton candy poof of synthetic hair.

"You didn't," I said, then paused. "I mean, mostly you didn't."

"I can't understand if you don't explain it, Cin."

I try to think of a way to explain my thoughts without it being insulting to all of us. I didn't want to believe they would whore themselves out to break their curse. I didn't want to think that they weren't attracted to me but were grasping at every chance to escape.

Worse, I was afraid that once the curse broke, they'd leave. I didn't want to be alone again. And they had no reason to stay. They didn't owe me anything, and I certainly didn't own them. But I enjoyed their company. I liked having them around.

Sure, they'd done some shady shit in their past. You didn't get cursed to over a hundred years of servitude if you didn't. But I liked the people they were now.

"Talk to me, Cin." Cy used his hand to lift my face to meet his gaze. I tried not to flinch.

"I don't want you to do anything you don't want to do." I blurted out, unable to take the weight of his gaze and the tremulous feelings inside me. "I don't want you to feel like you have to sleep with me because I'm lonely and pathetic and haven't gotten laid in a year. That can't be the answer to your curse."

"You think this is a pity fuck?" His hand slid down to my neck, where he wrapped his three blunt fingers around my throat. He didn't squeeze, but the firm pressure was enough to force my head back until he could bend down and seize my mouth in a scorching kiss.

It was unlike any kiss I'd ever had. His skin was

rubbery and hard. His mouth was cool, instead of the warmth I expected. But I didn't mind. Instead, when he thrust his tongue out to stroke mine, I met him stroke for stroke. I gripped my hands in his hair and tugged. I needed him closer.

Cy released my throat and moved his hands down to cup my ass and bring me higher up his body. My feet left the ground, and I clung to his shoulders for dear life.

He was large all over, wide and tall with tree-trunk legs and arms. I felt secure in his grasp as he continued to kiss the life out of me. I was gasping and panting when he finally pulled away.

"Does that feel like pity to you?"

I shook my head, completely unable to form words.

"If anything, you're doing me the favor. I haven't been able to fuck anyone in a century." He said.

"And I thought a year was bad," I joked, but not really. I couldn't imagine a century without sex.

Cy growled and kissed me again. I met him stroke for stroke. His hands kneaded my ass in my little shorts, and I wished they were gone so I could feel his touch on my flesh. I was already damp and needy.

The Trogg took a few steps forward, and suddenly I found myself on my feet beside the bed staring up at the large doll. I raked my eyes over him and paused when I reached the smooth curve of him between his legs.

There I was getting all hot and bothered and excited, and the poor guy doesn't even have a penis to dick me down with. Something must have shown on my face because Cy laughed and ran a hand over the spot where his dick should have been.

"Don't worry, Cin," his black eyes glittered with fire and dark amusement. "I can take care of you. You just have to be a good girl and do what I say. Can you do that?"

My heart thundered in my ears, and my pussy clenched. The former gifted and talented child turned ADHD burnout millennial in me went feral for praise. And the way the words slipped out of him was practically obscene.

I nodded, unable to form my own words. The inability seemed to please him as much as the agreement. His smile was fierce as he raked his eyes over me.

"Good," he yanked the top blankets off the bed and grinned. "Now get on the bed."

seven

. . .

I stared at the bed for a heartbeat. Was I really going to do this? I wasn't even entirely sure what 'this' entailed. The doll had no external parts that I could see. I guessed he had hands.

I glanced at his hand, large and thick. What would it feel like to have them on me? The rubbery plastic would slide against my skin. His fingers were thick and smooth. My pussy clenched around nothing as I thought about the feel of them inside of me.

On shaky legs, I climbed onto the bed and sat with my legs beneath me. My shorts had ridden up my thighs, and all but disappeared into the folds of my legs and belly.

My belly was round and firm. I thought of it like a watermelon and had more than once been congratulated on my non-existent pregnancy because of the shape and size of it. And it was completely on display at the moment. I crossed my arms over it to hide.

"No hiding." Cy's hands reached out to grip

mine and pull them down to my sides. "I want to see you."

His plasticy hands were cool as they brushed against the upper curve of my belly. They skimmed the lower curves of my breasts through my sports bra and I shivered at the cool touch.

"I'm not going to take anything you don't want to give." Cy's thick fingers worked their way under the sides of my bra and pulled. I hesitated before lifting my arms to help him remove the garment. "I'm going to need you to tell me what you like and don't like."

He dropped the bra to the floor and leaned back to just look at me. I struggled to keep my arms at my sides and not hide myself from his gaze. My boobs aren't especially large, not for my size, but they have never been perky either. They rest on top of my belly with light brown nipples pointing toward the floor.

"You are beautiful," Cy said, reaching out to brush a gentle finger down the curve of my breasts and circle a nipple. My skin tightened, and I shuddered under his cool touch.

"No false praise," I told him, not wanting pretty words that don't mean anything. "Only the truth between us."

He made a hum but didn't agree. His black eyes focused on the movement of his thick fingers around the sensitive tip of my breast.

"Cy doesn't lie." Amethyst's voice came from the doorway behind me. I nearly jumped and covered myself, but Cy gripped my arms and held me in place.

I craned my neck to look behind me, where Amethyst stood taking up the entire doorway with her broad Trogg frame and tuft of purple hair. She had her arms awkwardly crossed as she leaned against the frame.

"He's a bastard, but he's not a liar." She glanced at him and then back at me. "Is this a private party or can I join?"

Her voice was flippant, but there was an undertone of something that made me stop and look at her. She was the one to start things out in the living room, and then there I was with Cy, leaving her alone in the other room.

"Depends," I said. "Why do you want to?"

My voice didn't waver, but I felt the uncertainty throughout my entire body. Especially when Amethyst straightened from the doorframe, and entered the room.

"One," she said, as she reached the other side of the bed behind me. "I'm a spoiled brat who hates to be left out of things. Ask Cy, I was forever making the boys play with me as a kid."

"Two," she slid a cool plastic finger down my back. "I haven't touched or been touched by anyone in a century."

"Three," her broad fingers dipped into the waist of my shorts where they slid to just cover my ass. The tips brushed against my plump flesh, and I shuddered. "There is nothing hotter to me than making a beautiful woman fall apart."

She leaned forward until her lips brushed my ear. "And you, my lovely little Cin, would look so pretty in pieces under my hands."

I gasped and jerked forward. Cy was there, his hands gripped my arms to keep me in place.

"Oh, shit." I gasped and then shuddered as Amethyst's hands wrapped around my body to cup and knead my breasts. "Yes, please."

"Always have to upstage me, don't you?" Cy said and grinned at Amethyst over my shoulder.

I could feel Amethyst's grin against my cheek as she kneaded and toyed with my breasts. Cy's smile was soft as he slid his hands down my arms to my hips. He used his grip to pull me to my knees and slid my shorts down as far as they would go.

"Just be a good boy and get her pants off." Amethyst used her grip on my boobs to pull me up further, allowing Cy to help me maneuver onto my ass so he could pull my shorts down my legs. And just like that, I was naked in front of the two Troggs.

I squirmed in my seat and tried to keep my hands at my sides. Amethyst's hands left my breasts and skimmed over my belly to my thighs. Her wide hands spanned the tops of my legs and were strong enough to pull them apart in one move. I was too surprised to stop her, and Cy was immediately there. He used his broad frame to keep my legs wide.

"I've never touched anyone in this body," Amethyst said as she dragged her hand down my torso toward my mound. "We'll have to figure out what works together."

"Which means you have to tell us what you like and don't like," Cy said. He gripped my hips and held me in place while Amethyst's hand continued to head over the curve of my belly and down. "Can you do that, Cinny?"

I glared and reached up to grab a chunk of the Trogg's blue hair. "Don't call me Cinny."

Cy laughed, and I was about to tug again when Amethyst's hand found home and her fingers curled over my mound with the middle of the three pressing between my lips. It spanned the distance from my clit to just barely pressing against my opening and made me gasp.

"Don't be a brat, Cinder." Amethyst said into my cheek. "Brats don't get nice things."

Her finger slid down to press against my hole. She gave me the barest of friction before pulling away and moving her hand up to circle around my clit. The slick plastic felt different. Almost like the head of a dildo but firmer and more rounded.

Cy's hands lifted to pinch at my nipples. My nipples had two modes, completely dead or almost unbearably sensitive. Currently, they were the latter. The gentle pinches were enough to send me rocking against the dolls.

"So sensitive," Cy said, leaning down to take one nipple into his mouth. It was weird. Plasticy and cool. It wasn't bad, but it was different enough that I was able to come down a little bit.

"I don't think she likes that," Amethyst said, continuing her slow circling of my clit.

"It's weird," I admit. "Kind of what I imagine using a breast pump feels like."

"Kinky." Amethyst said with a laugh.

"Not mine." Kids and lactation kind of frightened me, to be honest. I pressed my hips against Amethyst's hand, begging for more friction, but she refused to give it to me.

"What is?" Cy asked, popping off of my nipple. His hands returned to my hips where he held me still for Amethyst's touch.

I don't say anything. Sure, I'm naked with both of them playing with my body, but I wasn't sure it was the right time to be talking about my kinks. We were friendly, but I didn't know them that well.

Amethyst slapped my pussy in one firm blow

that had me fighting against Cy's grip. I gasped as sensation flooded me.

"Answer Cy," Amethyst demanded before running her finger down my labia to my opening and back up again in soft, gentle strokes.

"I don't know." I said, unsure how much to admit. Most of my kinks were in theory. Sure, it sounded hot in books and movies, but did I actually want to be tied up and made to come until I passed out? Did being completely at someone's mercy actually feel as hot as it sounded?

"Liar," Cy chided, slapping my hip.

"I don't," I repeated. And then I sagged forward and admitted all of it. "I've only ever had pretty vanilla sex. I'm not sure what I actually like and what just sounds fun but I have a feeling they aren't always the same."

"You'd be right about that," Amethyst laughed. "No matter how fun it sounds, never get more partners than you have holes."

She shook out a wrist like it was sore, and I couldn't help but laugh. I wondered if she was exaggerating for my benefit or if she'd really had an orgy.

"I've never had more than one person at a time." I admitted. "And spanking is as crazy as I've ever gotten."

"Did you like it?" Cy asked, rubbing at my hips and down the outside of my thighs.

"Receiving. It felt weird giving."

"That's okay," Amethyst said against my neck. "I like giving."

Her mouth closed over my neck, and I moaned. A sound that ramped up when she finally, finally, slid a finger inside of me. Her hands were as large as Cy's and I'd been right. That one finger filled me as much as any dildo I owned.

"Keep going," Cy demanded. His black eyes bore into me as he gripped my knees and held them spread apart for Amethyst's touch.

"I don't know. Bondage sounds fun in theory, I guess." I lost focus for a moment when Amethyst hit my g-spot with her finger. She immediately pulled back, and I whined.

"Keep talking, pretty girl." Amethyst demanded. "Tell us what to do to you."

"I haven't had sex in a year. Just fuck me and I'll be over the moon." I writhed in their grips. I needed more touch. More friction. More everything.

"Pretty girl, you can get yourself off any time. I've seen your collection of delightful little toys. If we're going to do it, we're going to do it right."

Amethyst leaned forward and wrapped an arm around Cy's neck and pulled him in for a kiss. I was trapped between their bodies, cool plastic pinning me in place while Amethyst's finger remained buried deep inside of me.

"Okay, okay," I said as I wiggled my hips to get more friction where I needed it. "I like praise. I like the concept of sensory play but I'm actually super stressed about not being able to see what's coming. I think orgasm control and denial sounds pretty fucking hot but at the same time I'm pretty sure I would violently injure someone who kept me on edge for too long because I really love orgasms."

"Was that so hard?" Cy asked, pulling away from Amethyst. He leaned forward and planted his mouth on mine. The kiss was immediately deep and wet.

"Cy, be a good boy and get me the belt from the

pretty girl's robe." Amethyst said. She pulled her finger free of my body with a wet pop. Cy pulled away from me with a wide smile and left to his task.

Amethyst pressed her finger against my mouth, and I opened to taste myself. It was different than when past lovers had done it. The plastic made my taste stronger, since it wasn't mixed with the taste of my partner's skin. It wasn't bad, but I'd never loved tasting myself. I was just willing to do whatever Amethyst said if it got me closer to an orgasm.

My entire body hummed with anticipation and need. My pussy was clenching around nothing, and I didn't think it would take much effort at all to tip me over the edge.

Cy returned with the cotton belt to my sensible and boring cotton robe. Amethyst thanked him with another kiss and tugged the material straight in front of me.

"I'm going to tie your hands. If we do anything you don't like, tell us to stop. If you want us to untie you, just say so and I'll do it. Do you understand, pretty girl?" I nodded and, with a deep breath, moved my hands behind my back for Amethyst to tie.

My body was shaking by the time she was finished. Part anxiety, part arousal, I felt like I was crawling out of my skin.

"Are you okay?" Cy asked. "We can stop now. We don't have to do this."

"No," I shook my head and took a steadying breath. "I trust you. I'm just nervous."

"It's okay, pretty girl." Amethyst said, running her hands up my bound arms to my shoulders and down my chest to cup my breasts. She pressed up against the back of my body. "We're going to take good care of you."

She moved back and gently helped me lay back until my feet were dangling off the end of the bed with my feet near the floor. She was immediately there, between my legs.

"I'm going to make you feel so good," Amethyst promised me, running her hands up the inside of my thighs until her fingers were at the apex of my thighs.

She slid her finger up and down my seam, pressing a little deeper each time without ever actually touching my clit or core. I wiggled as much as I could, trying to get more friction but she just laughed and gave my pussy a little slap.

"Nuh-uh-uh, pretty girl. You have no say here. You're just going to lie there and take what we give you." My pussy clenched tight, and Amethyst laughed and looked to Cy. "Oh, she liked that."

"She's such a good girl," Cy said, stepping forward to run his fingers through my hair. "I can't wait to hear her beg."

I whimpered and shook in my bonds. It was too much. My heart was pounding in my chest, and I needed them to do something before I lost my mind.

"You wish is my command," Amethyst said before she pressed a finger deep inside of me.

eight

. . .

$\mathcal{I}$ screamed out and bowed off the bed at the unexpected, deep penetration. Amethyst immediately withdrew and pressed deep again. And again. I was a panting, whining mess in moments.

And then she stopped.

"Oh, sweet girl, it isn't going to be that easy." Amethyst said with a grin.

"Bitch," I spat back. My pussy was an aching mess. My breath was coming in pants. And I was about out of my mind with frustrated pleasure.

"Well, that's no way for a lady to talk. Cy, do something with that mouth." I glanced at the blue-haired Trogg and wondered exactly what he was going to do about it.

It didn't take long for me to learn. He climbed on top of me and straddled my head. Because his knees didn't bend very well, it was an awkward movement that distracted me from my aching cunt for a moment. But then Amethyst was there again, sliding her finger in deep and twisting it against my g-spot.

I arched up and snapped my eyes to where Cy

was standing over me. There, between his legs, was a perfectly round hole roughly the size of a baseball. I was about to ask about it when something came through the hole. It was the same tan tone as his skin and kind of looked like an oversized hot dog at first. And then I realized what it was and what Cy had meant earlier when he said he could take care of me. He had a cock pocket hiding this massive meat stick away. It grew until it was roughly half the length of his leg. It was long and smooth without a flared head and really did remind me of a hot dog. Or more accurately, at that size, a broomstick.

With him half-kneeling, half-crouched over my face, it was at the perfect length for him to grab it and direct it at my mouth. There, at the end, was a small hole where I supposed his cum came out. It was hands down the weirdest thing I'd ever seen and yet, I wanted my mouth on it.

I wanted to know what it would feel and taste like. I was practically ready to beg for it when he brushed the tip against my mouth. I opened immediately and began bobbing my head.

"God, she's an eager little thing." Cy groaned from above me.

"She's perfect," Amethyst said. She slid her finger back inside of me and began fucking me in a steady rhythm that matched the speed I bobbed on Cy's cock.

And Cy's cock. It was perfectly smooth on my tongue. Sure, it tasted a little plasticy but it was more rubbery than the rest of him. It felt not unlike sucking on one of my dildos. If my dildo was smooth, perfectly rounded, and tasted weirdly like cotton candy.

I wanted to ask about the flavor when Amethyst

pulled out and pushed back in with two fingers. I arched and screamed around Cy's cock. I clenched hard around her broad digits, coming instantly.

"Fuck," Cy groaned above me. "Make her do that again."

"My pleasure," Amethyst said. She fucked me slowly, stretching me out on her digits as she drove me back up to the edge again. This time, my orgasm was a slow build. One that came over me in a crashing wave.

I gasped and moaned around Cy's giant hot dog dick. The smooth plastic went completely still in my mouth before it began spurting cum down my throat. I swallowed greedily, loving the cotton candy taste of it. There was too much for me to take it all, and it leaked out of my mouth, down the sides of my face and onto my chest.

Amethyst pulled her fingers free of my pussy with a squelching sound that would have embarrassed me if I wasn't so completely blitzed out on orgasms and cotton candy cum. But I could do nothing but lay there and pant as Cy's cock retreated back into his body.

"How you doing, pretty girl?" Amethyst asked, soothing her hands up my legs and over my sides. "Still with us?"

"Can't feel my anything." I admit, still trying to catch my breath. "Sleep now."

"Not yet, doll." Cy said, awkwardly climbing off the bed. "Let's get you cleaned up first."

Amethyst and Cy helped me into a sitting position. Cy disappeared into the hallway while Amethyst untied my arms and helped rub them until blood flow returned properly. While she was doing that, Cy came back with a washcloth in hand.

He and Amethyst worked together to clean the

pearlescent cum off of my skin. I couldn't help but laugh and make a joke about my skin never looking more luminous.

Cy pulled off the sheet while Amethyst got a clean one, and they tucked me into bed still naked. I normally would put on a sleep shirt or shorts and a cami, but I was too tired and my entire body was languid.

"I know there's not a lot of space but could you stay with me? Just for a little while?" I felt awkward asking, but I was feeling raw and needed their company. I needed to know this wasn't just about breaking the curse.

"Of course, doll." Cy said, rolling onto the bed facing me. I rolled toward him and put my arm around his waist. Amethyst came up behind me and tucked her arm around me. It was warm in the cocoon of my blankets, their bodies were a firm pressure against my exhausted body. And it didn't take long for me to drift off.

nine

. . .

woke to sweltering heat. The Troggs had been cool on the outside of my blankets and had kept the temperature comfortable all night as I slept, but now I was sweating. I grumbled and tried to work my way out of the blankets, but they were pinned on either side of me. I pushed against the weight and got a grumbled male response in return.

The Troggs had stayed all night. I tightened my arm around Cy but it wasn't smooth plastic under my hand but warm flesh. My eyes flew open at the same time his did. Instead of the deep black glass eyes I was used to, I found myself looking into deep set hazel eyes.

"Cy?" I asked, not quite believing what I was seeing. His soft mouth broke into a wide grin when he saw his arm. I looked down at my waist and the slender, feminine arm draped over it and laughed.

"Amethyst, wake up girl! We're back!" Cy jumped from the bed and danced around the room. Amethyst screamed and rolled off the bed onto the floor. I sat up and hauled the blankets up to my chest as I watched Cy help her up.

He pulled her into his arms and spun her around the room. He planted a big, smacking kiss to her mouth before spinning them around again. I watched them as they danced and talked animatedly to each other, my heart both elated and sinking.

They were back. The curse was broken. There was no reason for them to stay here. With me.

"Look at this, Cin!" Cy said, twirling Amethyst around. Both of them were so completely oblivious to their nudity, and I envied that comfort and freedom. "Isn't my best friend fucking gorgeous?"

She was. Of course she was. She was the quintessential 1920's lady with chin-length blond waves and wide blue eyes. Her waist was nipped in at her hips, and her boobs were so fucking perky they could take an eye out. I wanted to hate her. Except I was so happy for her.

Cy, still dancing around like a crazy person, had a lean swimmer's body. His sandy brown hair and deep hazel eyes were just the start of the movie star perfect package. Plus, his cock was so big I wondered how he wasn't hurting himself waving it around like that.

"Come, dance with us!" Amethyst said, holding out a beckoning hand. I just shook my head. "Cinder."

"I can't. I'm sorry. I'm so happy that you're back and the curse is broken. I'm so happy for you. It's great. Just wonderful." My voice broke on the last word, and the sadness that had been tugging at my heart broke loose. Sobs wracked my body as I buried my face in the blanket to hide.

Arms wrapped around me from both sides, and I was suddenly cocooned in warmth again. The blanket was tugged from my hand, and my face was pressed against a hard, warm chest.

I inhaled and smelled cotton candy. Which only made me giggle-sob messily into Cy's chest.

"Talk to us, doll." Cy's arms wrapped around me from one side. Amethyst wrapped around me from the other with her face buried in my neck.

"I-I-I just don't want you to leave," I blubbered.

Amethyst brushed a soft hand down my hair with a little sigh. "Oh, pretty girl, we're not going anywhere."

"We're happy to be back, but we want to be here with you." Cy's grip tightened around me.

"You don't have to, you know." I sniffled and pulled away to look at them. "I understand, you just got your lives back. And I'm sure you feel some sort of way about me but you don't have to stay just because I'm a mess."

"Pretty girl, we're not staying for you. We're staying because of you." Amethyst gently gripped my face and turned me to look at her. "Because of the way you took care of us, helped us, cared for us. I'm pretty sure no one has ever cared enough to actually help us our entire lives."

"I'm sure that's not true," I didn't want it to be true. It was heartbreaking, if it was.

"Don't feel bad for us," Cy said, pressing a kiss to my shoulder. "We were poor little rich kids, too selfish and entitled to know what we were missing. Until you. You could have kicked us out. You could have thrown us in the trash. Instead, you made us feel like we mattered again."

Amethyst ran her hands, small, dainty, and so different from the ones that had fucked me senseless the night before, down my arms to take my hands. She used our linked hands to wrap both of our arms around me in a hug.

"If you don't want us, we'll understand." Amethyst said, holding me tight. "But we want to stay with you."

My heart hammered in my chest. No one ever wanted to stay with me. My grandparents had spent my young years calling me a mistake and an accident. My mother had left as soon as I was old enough to abandon. Moved in with her new husband and just didn't have room for me anymore. Endless partners who never thought I was enough or insisted I was too much.

"Let us keep you," Cy said, wrapping his arms around Amethyst and I.

Tears were still falling when I gave in. Into the belief that someone could want me. Into the hope that they would stay. Into the comfort they offered. Just into them.

Cy's mouth met mine in a kiss that was so different from the one we shared the night before. This one was hot, wet. He probed deeply and devoured me. Amethyst released my hands and began pulling the blanket down and off of me. Cy's hands gripped my hips and pulled me up and onto him until I was straddling his legs. His cock nestled between us, and I couldn't help but pull back and look down at it.

"I thought it was a Trogg thing," I said, eyeing the large cock in front of me. This one was decidedly more human but still almost worryingly large.

"No doll, that is all me." He reached down and stroked his cock. He pumped twice before circling his thumb over the head and picking up the drop of cum beading there.

He brought his hand to my lips and pressed his

thumb against my mouth. I opened for him, tasting him. I expected it to taste like normal but pulled back when the taste of cotton candy blossomed on my tongue.

"You still taste like candy," I exclaimed. Cy's eyebrows drew together. "Your cum tastes like cotton candy. You didn't know that?"

"Um, pretty sure it didn't used to." Cy said with a frown.

"Definitely not," Amethyst said, tossing the blanket away. "I would have been more willing to suck your cock if it tasted like candy."

I looked between them. I guessed it made sense that they'd been together. They were far too comfortable being naked together and being in bed together for two people who had never fucked. But I just hadn't really thought about it.

"Does that bother you?" Amethyst asked, crawling over to straddle Cy's lap behind me. She set her hands on my hips. "That we've been together?"

"No, I just didn't expect it. Which is dumb. I mean, look at you. Of course you've had sex." My voice wasn't very convincing. I shook my head and tried again. "It doesn't bother me. It just surprised me, which is dumb."

"Not dumb," Cy said. He wrapped a hand around the back of my neck and pulled me in for a kiss. Amethyst's mouth pressed against my shoulder blade.

"It wasn't a thing. It was just… a thing. You know?" She pressed another kiss to my shoulder. "Stupid things that stupid kids do."

Cy released me and turned my head so Amethyst could press a kiss to my lips. Kissing her was softer, gentler, and no less thrilling than kissing

Cy. Cy, whose hand was dipping between my legs to circle my clit with his thumb.

I squeaked and jumped when he made contact. They both laughed. Amethyst's hands went to my hips to hold me in place.

"So responsive," Cy said, doing it again. I whimpered and pressed against him. "I want to taste you, doll. Will you let me?"

Oral wasn't something I normally did. One, because few men bothered to offer. Two because being splayed out like that made me feel like a beached whale, and I could never get out of my head enough to enjoy it. But Cy and Amethyst hadn't criticized my body and seemed to like how I looked. It would be okay.

I nodded.

"We need your words, pretty girl."

"Yes," I whispered the word. But it was enough. Amethyst crawled off of Cy's lap and pulled me back until I was lying back on Cy's legs with my legs spread to either side of his hips.

Soft fingers slid down my labia in a gentle caress. I tried to keep my legs open as those fingers spread me open, exposing all of me. "So pretty."

I was ready to argue when Amethyst leaned over me and pressed her lips to mine. It was a gentle caress, one that matched the soft touches on my lower lips.

My hips squirmed in Cy's hold. I felt awkward and exposed. I couldn't focus on my discomfort though because Amethyst was kissing me in earnest now. Her hand moved down to cup my breast.

Cy gripped my hips and lifted them up until he could lean over and press a kiss to my mound. His lips slid down until they covered all of me.

Gentle, wet licks everywhere except where I needed him.

My hands clenched in the covers for a moment before I released them and reached for Amethyst. I wanted to touch her too. She hadn't gotten any pleasure the night before, and I wanted to make up for that lapse.

She pulled away to look into my eyes as my hands explored her torso and hips. Everything I could get my hands on with her above my head and Cy holding my hips two feet off the ground.

"Come here," I begged her. "Let me make you feel good too."

"Making you feel good makes me feel good." Amethyst said, before she ran her fingers down my torso to circle my hard nipples. "Cy, stop teasing her."

"Bossy," he grumbled against my pussy. The vibration was new and strange and had me bucking up.

"Make her come or I won't let you come."

"And mean," Cy said. But he apparently took her threat seriously because the teasing licks and nips stopped and he began to work me with his tongue with wicked determination.

"Let go, pretty girl. Just feel." Amethyst said, teasing my nipples with gentle tugs and rolls. She was bossy. But she wasn't the only one who could demand what she wanted.

I reached above my head and wrapped my arms around her thighs until I could pull her forward. She stumbled forward on her knees until she was right over my face. I tugged her down until I could smell her. She smelled like bubble gum. The kind I got as a kid by the bucket that was hard to chew and lost its flavor in minutes.

Wondering if she tasted as sweet as she smelled, I tugged a little bit more until her soft curls brushed my skin and I could bury my face in her folds.

"Fuck, look who's bossy now," Amethyst said, gripping my boobs like handlebars.

She tasted like bubble gum. I couldn't explain it, and I didn't really care. She was fucking delicious, and she was all mine.

Cy's tongue dipped inside of me, and I gasped into Amethyst's pussy. She gasped above me and moved her hips, grinding down on my face.

"Make her do it again," she demanded of Cy. Her hands went back to toying with my breasts. Cy didn't hesitate to listen. He moved his attention up to my clit and sucked hard until I was bucking and writhing in his grasp.

Between the pleasure and the pussy on my face, I was panting for breath. For one terrifying moment, I thought I was going to pass out, then Cy sucked hard on my clit, using just a bit of teeth, and I flew apart.

I screamed into Amethyst's pussy, causing her to moan and grind faster. Cy lowered my hips back to his lap, and I collapsed.

"I was so close," Amethyst whined. She scooted back off my head and looked down at me. "How are you doing, pretty girl?"

I gave a weak thumbs up, and mustered up a smile. I couldn't feel anything below my waist, and my legs wouldn't stop shaking.

"Oh, I'm not done with her yet." Cy said before sliding out from underneath me. He flipped me over and raised my hips back into the air. At least this time it was a better angle, and I wasn't being bowed backward.

"Do you want this?" He asked, brushing the

head of his cock over my sensitive, wet flesh. "Are you ready to take my cock, doll?"

I whimpered, uncertain if I was capable of taking the giant appendage, but fuck, I was going to try.

"Yes, I want it. I want you." The words came out hoarse but steady, and it was enough. Cy slid his cock down until the head was notched at my opening.

"Oh, no, condom!" I scrambled up and started digging through my bedside table. I was certain I had some in there from the last attempt at dating a few months before.

I had no clue if he could get me pregnant. Twenty-four hours ago he was a Trogg doll, and he still had cum that tasted like cotton candy. I had no clue what the rules were, but I was not risking an unwanted pregnancy. I wouldn't pass that legacy on to a child.

Finally, I found the box that I never even opened and checked the date. I let out a little yip of relief when I saw they weren't expired. I tore into the box and handed one of the packets to Cy.

He looked at it with disgust. "Must we?"

"Hey, I don't know what type of condoms you had back in 1902 but today's are barely there. You'll be fine." I took the condom back and ripped the packet open before reaching for Cy's cock to roll it on.

"I am capable of doing that."

"Yeah, but it's more fun if I do it." I pinched the tip and rolled the condom down his cock, and down. And down. I wasn't actually sure how effective it was going to be. There was a lot of cock left over at the end of the condom.

"Are we sure this thing is going to fit?"

"Haven't had a problem yet. Now bend over for me and let me fuck you."

"Isn't he cute when he gets bossy?" Amethyst asked. I turned toward her and grinned.

"You're both cute when you're bossy."

"I'm about to be the cutest." She waited until I was back on my elbows and knees, ready to take Cy's cock, before she slid her way down the bed. She laid spread out in front of me, legs open and pussy shining with a mixture of my saliva and her essence. "I want you to finish me while he fucks you. Think you can focus that long?"

No, I absolutely did not. But I was going to try. I wrapped my arms around her legs and dipped my head to take her clit into my mouth. At her first moan, Cy pressed inside of me.

He wasn't particularly thick, but he was long, so long. He kept pressing deeper and deeper and I was certain he'd have to stop at some point. There was a limit to what I could take. But he kept pushing, and my body kept adjusting to accept him.

By the time he was fully seated inside me, my legs were shaking and I wasn't sure how much more I could take before I came apart again.

I'd never been a multiples type of girl. It was usually one and done for me, but my body was already on the verge and he hadn't done anything but slide inside.

The tip of his cock pressed against my cervix with a pressure that had me squirming and moaning into Amethyst's cunt. I could feel him so deep inside of me it was almost painful. Almost.

"Tell me if it gets to be too much, doll." And then he was moving. He thrust in slow, shallow movements that had me clenching. I tried to pay attention to giving Amethyst the pleasure she deserved, but my eyes were crossing with the feeling of Cy's cock inside of me.

Amethyst had her hands clenched in my hair as she directed me where she wanted me. I slid two fingers inside of her and curled until I pressed against the soft spot that would drive her insane. She yelled out and bucked against my face. I pressed and curled faster while lapping at her clit.

All the while, Cy was picking up speed, sending me forward into Amethyst's pussy with every thrust. My entire body was vibrating with pleasure and sensation. It was all too much. The stretch in my pussy, the hands tugging on my hair, the sweet bubble gum taste of Amethyst. Cy's grip on my hips was bruising and when he slid one hand down and over until he could press against my clit.

It was all over then. I screamed into Amethyst's pussy at the same time she arched into my face and clenched around my fingers. I bucked against Cy's grip as I clenched around him. With one final, brutal thrust, Cy came. I could feel the spray of his cum inside of me and knew the condom hadn't made it.

I made a mental note to get some Plan B from the store before I collapsed on top of Amethyst with my head on her stomach. She ran fingers through my damp hair as Cy collapsed on top of both of us.

"Ugh, get off." Amethyst pushed at his shoulder, and he rolled over on the bed to lay next to us. His hand came to my back to smooth up and down the expanse of skin. I was too tired and sated to even think about the fact I was probably squishing Amethyst.

Eventually, Cy got up to deal with the damaged condom. He came back with two warm, damp cloths. He handed one to Amethyst before gently rolling me over and cleaning me up from the cum on my face down to the cum leaking out of me.

It was nice to be taken care of. I tried not to enjoy it too much. I didn't want to get used to it, but a part of me, for just one moment, wished that I could keep this forever.

Cy and Amethyst curled up around me until we were in a cuddle pile in the middle of my too-small bed. Even though it was still morning, I let myself drift off to sleep and dream of a life where people didn't leave me.

ten

. . .

I woke up alone. I wasn't surprised, but it didn't stop the stab of hurt. I'd thought that maybe this time would be different. At least for a little while, I'd hoped they would stay.

My stomach forced me out of bed. I tried to find my robe, but it was nowhere to be seen. So, I pulled on a pair of underwear and an oversized t-shirt and headed out to the kitchen.

I stopped dead just outside the bedroom door. There they were. Cy and Amethyst were sitting on the couch. Amethyst was wearing my robe, and Cy had on a pair of old workout shorts that were far too small and absolutely obscene. They both looked over when I came out and smiled.

Cy jumped up off of the couch and rushed to the kitchen. "Coffee? We made a pot not long ago. I have pancakes and bacon for breakfast. The bacon is warming and the batter is ready so just say the word."

He was talking too fast and seemed a little nervous. Which was weird because Cy had never seemed anything but confident.

"Breakfast sounds great." I joined him in the

kitchen to make my coffee, but he was already pouring some into a mug and had the chocolate creamer I liked out.

He spun around to turn on the stove, and I stopped him with a hand on his arm. "Are you okay?"

"He's worried you're going to kick us out," Amethyst said, coming into the kitchen behind me. "I know you said you wanted us to stay. But, well. . ."

She trailed off with a shrug. And I looked between them, absolutely dumbstruck. They were worried I was kicking them out? It seemed insane. But then I thought about it, and it made sense. They needed me. They were out of their time and had nothing.

Was that why they wanted to stay? Because they had nothing else? Gah! I hated second guessing every word and thought. I wanted them here. They wanted to be here. It didn't have to be so difficult.

"I'm not sending you anywhere. We'll figure it out." I squeezed Cy's arm before turning to look at Amethyst. "As long as you want to stay, you're more than welcome to be here."

She gave me a sweet smile before wrapping me up in a hug. Cy's arms came around me from the back and enclosed both of us. We stood there for a long moment, swaying in the three way hug.

I had no clue how I was going to reasonably support three people. I had a decent income, but it definitely wasn't enough to support three adults. And it wasn't like two people born in 1900 could exactly go get jobs.

Cy pulled away to start my breakfast, and Amethyst leaned around me to grab my coffee mug before pulling me back to the couch. As I settled in

Amethyst curled around me, I decided it would be a problem for another day.

Sure, there was a lot to figure out, but nothing was insurmountable. And maybe this time, they would stay. Maybe this time I wouldn't be left on my own again.

Breakfast was a quiet affair with all of us piled on the couch together watching an action movie. Amethyst sat leaning against my shoulder with her feet in Cy's lap. It was comfortable and cozy, and I never wanted it to end.

They seemed to agree because by unspoken agreement we did nothing but lay around, have sex, and enjoy being with each other all day Saturday.

When we fell into bed in a sweaty, exhausted heap that night, I couldn't think of anywhere I'd rather be.

eleven

. . .

"We have got to get you some clothes," I said Sunday morning over omelets and orange juice. Cy turned out to be a pretty decent cook for someone who had never cooked a day before in his life. Even better, he actually liked it.

I hooked him up with my laptop to search for recipes. After he figured out the technology, he went hog wild writing down recipes and making shopping lists.

Which brought me back to my main point, we had to get them some clothes. Cy was nearly six feet tall, and nothing I had even remotely fit him. He was too tall, too slender, too well-endowed for anything I owned. And Amethyst hadn't been able to fit into anything but my robe.

The biggest challenge was that they had no concept of their sizes, so I couldn't even just go grab something from the local super store. Not that they were keen on letting me out of the house without them.

"I don't understand why," Amethyst said, tugging at the hem of my shirt. "We could all just stay naked forever and solve the problem."

"Well, I have to go to work for one." I said, pushing her hands away. I would not be distracted again. "And Cy wants to get groceries for another and he cannot go out in those."

He wore a pair of my sweats that were about six inches too short, and even tied, hung dangerously low on his hips. He hadn't bothered with a shirt, and while I wouldn't complain about the view, he needed clothes. They both did.

We were still debating about it when my phone rang and Abury's name came up. I answered right away. We did not call each other. We texted. Phone calls meant emergencies.

"Hey, what's wrong?" I said, immediately preparing to leave the house.

"Hopefully nothing. I got a weird call today. Do you remember the vintage store I bought your dolls from? Well, they asked that you bring them back in."

I looked at the humans that used to be Troggs, and my heart rate kicked up. I couldn't imagine why they'd want them back, but it wasn't happening. Even if I could, I wouldn't.

"I can't do that," I told my best friend. I wanted to tell her more, everything. But how could she possibly believe me?

"Addy was pretty insistent that they come back."

"Addy?"

"She's one of the owners at Retro Whimsy. She's super nice and I'm sure it's nothing but you should go."

"Aubry, I can't." I took a deep breath and decided to just get into it. "They're gone."

Aubry screeched into the phone, and there was

a masculine rumble on the other side. "Nothing, Leo. Go tell Markus to calm down. I'm fine."

"How many men do you have over there?" I knew she was seeing someone new, but she never said there were multiple someones. Then again, I hadn't told her about having two life-sized dolls. Some things were too weird even for your best friend.

"Three, I'll tell you about it later. First, please tell me you don't have the Troggs because they're incredibly sexy men and not because you tossed them out."

I blinked. And blinked again. I wasn't even sure how to respond to that. She was almost spot on.

"Halfway right." I mumbled, trying to make sense of her guess.

"Did you throw them out?" She sounded absolutely shocked and scandalized.

"No!" I shot back, horrified at the idea. "It's not two men."

"Hot." Was all she said. Then she giggled. "Julain, stop it. I'll be done in a minute."

I guess she wasn't joking about the three men, and I needed the details there immediately. But when I demanded information, she waved me off. "I'll tell you at lunch tomorrow. But go into the store today. Take your people. It'll be okay. Trust me."

"You gave me cursed dolls and are living a secret life. I'm not sure it would be wise to do that."

"Fuck you, bestie. Go to the store." She squealed and said a hurried goodbye before hanging up with a laugh.

I looked up from my phone to find both Cy and Amethyst staring at me. They both had guarded looks on their faces, and I hated it. I sighed and put my phone aside.

"That was my bestie, the one who bought you from the store. She said we have to go back there."

"I don't want to," Amethyst said right away. She looked nervous, and I couldn't blame her. I'd be worried about it too after spending a hundred years cursed. The timing was suspicious, with the curse breaking less than forty-eight hours earlier.

"Me either," Cy said, reaching out to take Amethyst's hand. "But I think we have to. Maybe they can tell us something about why we're back and make sure we get to stay this way."

"I'll leave it up to you," I said. It wasn't my life on the line, and I wouldn't sway them. They shared a look that was filled with a hundred years of friendship and a million words.

"Okay, let's do this." Amethyst said, reaching for me. "Let's get it behind us."

twelve

. . .

$\mathcal{I}$ found a pair of men's sweats that I forgot I owned because they were too long. They were still too large for Cy but they at least reached his ankles. He wore one of my shirts that was far too baggy for him. Which fit perfectly with Amethyst, who was drowning in one of my dresses. Her lean frame disappeared into my plus-sized cotton dress, but it was enough. She was able to wear a pair of my sandals, though her heels hung over the back a little.

We stopped at a dollar store, and I bought a pair of cheap flip-flops for Cy. They were ugly and cheap, but they would do until we could get to a real store and get some clothes. I wanted to do that first, but they insisted on getting the trip to Retro Whimsy behind us.

"We don't have to do this," I told them, standing outside the free-standing vintage store in Old Town. Cy gripped my hand with a little too much force. I imagined he did the same to Amethyst on the other side. He was vibrating with tension.

"Yes, we do." His voice was far more sure than I

imagined he felt. But he took a step forward, and Amethyst and I immediately fell into pace. "It'll be fine."

I tried to release his hand to open the door, but he refused to let go. So, I pulled it open with my free hand and waited for them to maneuver through it while keeping us all linked. The bell on the door gave a cheery little ring, and something in me wanted to pull them out of there before anyone saw us.

"Welcome to Retro Whimsy."

I looked to the counter where a young woman manned the register. She was tall with long black hair. She wore a cut black t-shirt and a dark red and black plaid skirt. I wasn't sure if I wanted to be her or kiss her.

"Hi, my friend Aubry said you called." I gave an awkward wave, unsure what to do with my hand. I wanted to slap myself and immediately shoved my hand into my dress pocket to keep from flailing.

"Oh, right. Cool." She looked at my partners, and I wanted to step in front of them. "Welcome back. I have something for you."

She disappeared behind some black curtains, and the three of us exchanged looks. Cy and Amethyst didn't know what to make of her any more than I did. Before we could say anything, the woman was coming back. She carried a wooden box the size of a shoe box.

"We obviously had to change a few details but there's everything you need to survive in the modern world. Please try not to piss off any more witches. We won't be able to give you a third chance."

Cy and Amethyst shared a look before she

reached for the box. She handed Cy the lid before flipping through the paperwork. I leaned over Cy to look into the box. Inside there were passports, birth certificates, and driver's licenses. Everything they'd need to get jobs and move about society.

"How? Why?" I asked, completely confused about how they'd known, had managed to create this paperwork trail that shouldn't exist.

"Does it really matter?" The girl grinned, her teeth flashing white against her blood red lipstick. "You've got everything you've ever wanted, they're back to their original forms. Does the how or why really matter?"

I wanted to say yes, it did matter. That I needed to know how this was possible. I needed to know why she cared enough to do it. But I had other things to worry about. They had everything they needed to exist without me. What was there to keep them here?

As if sensing the direction my thoughts had taken, Cy turned to me with a grin. "Looks like we really do need to go clothes shopping."

He slung an arm around my shoulders and hugged me close. Amethyst looked at me with so much joy in her expression, I couldn't say anything. I was not going to ruin their moment. No, I was going to choose to believe that they wanted me and that they would stay.

They didn't have to need me to want to be with me. And I would have to learn to believe that. Because I wanted them. Both of them were already mine.

"I guess we do," I said with a grin. I turned back to the pretty alt girl and nodded. "Thank you for giving them their lives back."

"Oh, I didn't do that. You did that together.

We're just giving them a second chance to be better people. Enjoy it."

Cy and Amethyst continued to go through the box as we walked out the door. "What's this?" Amethyst asked, holding up a debit card.

"It's money." I looked in the box and found an envelope from a bank. I opened it and tripped on the sidewalk. "A whole fucking lot of money."

I gaped at the number of the balance sheet in front of me. It was more money than I would make in multiple lifetimes. "What did you say you did before you were cursed?"

"We were just spoiled kids. But my dad was in oil. Cy's dad did something with banking. Must be our inheritance." She shrugged as though seeing millions of dollars was totally normal thing.

"Here I was worried about feeding all of us."

"Now you don't have to worry about a single thing." Amethyst pressed a quick kiss to my lips. "Let's go shopping!"

epilogue

...

"You told them too much, Lacey." The tall red-head said, stepping through the black curtains onto the main floor of Retro Whimsy. She stepped to the counter until she could watch the throuple walk down the sidewalk toward the public parking lot.

"I didn't tell them shit," The black-haired woman spat back. "They have no clue what happened. Chill out, Chloe."

"No one can know what we're doing here," Chloe said. She looked around the careful collection of items that filled their vintage store. Some of them were perfectly normal items. But others, they were special.

"If you have a problem with how I handle things, make Addy do it. Even better, do it yourself." Lacey eyed her nails and frowned at a chip in the black polish. "No one is going to figure it out. Least of all a couple of spoiled kids and a clueless human."

"Lacey," Chloe started, but her sister cut her off.

"Chloe, it's fine. No one will figure it out. We've been planning this for centuries. We know what we're doing." Lacey reached out and put a hand on her sister's arm.

The three sisters couldn't have been more different. But they all agreed on one thing: their mission. And none of them would mess it up.

"Who's next?" Lacey asked.

"Addy wouldn't say." Chloe began playing with jewelry under the glass counter. Nothing was out of place, but Lacey knew her sister liked to tweak things when she got nervous. And they were all nervous these days.

"Brat." Lacey's voice was amused more than heated. "Let's hope it happens soon."

"What do you know?" Chloe stopped fidgeting and looked to her sister. Lacey's expression turned inward clearly focused on something Chloe couldn't see.

"Just that we're running out of time."

"Well, we'll help as many of them as we can before we do."

"Let's hope it will be enough."

about the author

Sabrina Cross (she/her) is a neurospicy 80's baby from the middle of nowhere Michigan, where she still lives with her cat. She came into her monster romance era early when she fell in love with Beast from the 1997's X-Men animated series. After discovering sentient object romance in early 2023, Sabrina decided to embrace what she calls her 'Hold My Beer' style of writing and gave into the lifelong dream of being an author. When not writing weird monster/sentient object smut, Sabrina can be found hanging out on social media (@authorsabrinacross), reading, or hoarding office supplies.

also by sabrina cross

Yarn & Monsters Series

A True Love Spell Gone Wrong...

When four friends perform a true love spell, things go terribly wrong. Now they're locked into a deal with the devil and have only a year to find love and happiness or their souls are destined to face the flames. Armed with a demon guardian; Clover, Jasmine, Fern, and Violet are determined to beat the devil and save themselves. Except, this curse might be the best thing that's ever happened to them.

Corny: A F/F Candy Corn Romance

Snuggle: A M/F Demon Teddy Bear Romance

Tangled: A M/F Friends-To-Lovers Sentient Object Romance

Knotted: A M/F Demon Werewolf Romance

The Cursed Matchmaker Series

Never Piss off a witch. Or else you may find yourself trapped in a glory hole booth at an upscale sex club. But when the perfect couples hook up anonymously, Josh has no choice but to speak out and help them find love.

The Glory Whole Package

The Glory Whole Experiment

The Glory Whole Redemption

Retro Whimsy Series

Welcome to Retro Whimsy where nothing is as it seems and the owners know just what you need.

Getting Railed

Trogg Trouble

Ghostlight Falls - Shared World Series

Cooking Up A Demon

Stand Alone Monster Romance

Christmas with the Monster

Can't Yeti Enough

Stand Alone Sentient Object Romance

Light Me Up

Pounded by the Pommel Horse

Sentient Pen15 from Outer Space

Knotty Broomsticks